TURN! TURN! TURN! TURN! TURN! TURN! TURN! TURN! TURN! TURN! TURN! TURN! TURN! TURN! TURN! TURN! TURN!

To every thing there is a season,
and a time to every purpose under the heaven:

a time to be born, and a time to die;
a time to plant, and a time to pluck up that which is planted;

a time to kill, and a time to heal;
a time to break down, and a time to build up;

a time to weep, and a time to laugh;
a time to mourn, and a time to dance;

a time to cast away stones, and a time to gather stones together;
a time to embrace, and a time to refrain from embracing;

a time to get, and a time to lose;
a time to keep, and a time to cast away;

a time to rend, and a time to sew;
a time to keep silence, and a time to speak;

a time to love, and a time to hate;
a time of war, and a time of peace.

—from the book of Ecclesiastes
in the King James Version of the Bible

TURN! TU

WORDS FROM **ECCLESIASTES** קהלת CIRCA 250 B.C.E. · TRANSLATED INTO ENGLISH IN 1607

ILLUSTRATED IN 2003 BY **WENDY ANDERSON HALPERIN**

Simon & Schuster Books for Young Readers

RN! TURN! TURN!

ARRANGED AND ADAPTED WITH MUSIC IN 1961 BY PETE SEEGER

READ BY YOU TODAY

New York · London · Toronto · Sydney · Singapore

To those people young and old throughout the world who are
bringing folks together from North, South, East, and West
— *P. S.*

To bluebirds in the spring
— *W. H.*

SIMON & SCHUSTER BOOKS FOR YOUNG READERS
An imprint of Simon & Schuster Children's Publishing Division
1230 Avenue of the Americas, New York, New York 10020
"Turn! Turn! Turn! (To Everything There Is a Season)"
Words from the book of Ecclesiastes
Adaptation and music by Pete Seeger
TRO-©-copyright 1962 (renewed) Melody Trails, Inc., New York, NY
Used by permission
Illustrations copyright © 2003 by Wendy Anderson Halperin
SIMON & SCHUSTER BOOKS FOR YOUNG READERS is a trademark of Simon & Schuster.
Book design by Greg Stadnyk
The text for this book is set in Brighton.
The illustrations for this book are rendered in watercolor and pencil.
Manufactured in China
2 4 6 8 10 9 7 5 3 1
Library of Congress Cataloging-in-Publication Data
Seeger, Pete, 1919-
Turn! turn! turn! : words from Ecclesiastes circa 250 B.C.E., translated into English in London in 1607 / arranged and adapted with music in 1961 by Pete Seeger ;
illustrated by Wendy Anderson Halperin.
p. cm.
Includes one sound disc (digital ; 4 3/4 in.) of music.
Summary: A song, based on Bible verses, which proclaims that there is a season for everything, as well as the original music by Pete Seeger, The Byrds' version of
the tune, and notes by Seeger about writing the song.
ISBN 0-689-85235-5
1. Folk songs, English—United States. [1. Folk songs—United States. 2. Songs.] I. Halperin, Wendy Anderson, ill. II. Title.
PZ8.3.S4505 Tu 2003
[782.42]—dc21
2002154855

To everything turn, turn, turn there is a season turn, turn, turn and a time for every purpose under heaven.

BORN

A time to be born

a time to die

a time to reap

a time to kill

a time to heal

LAUGH

A time to laugh

a time to weep

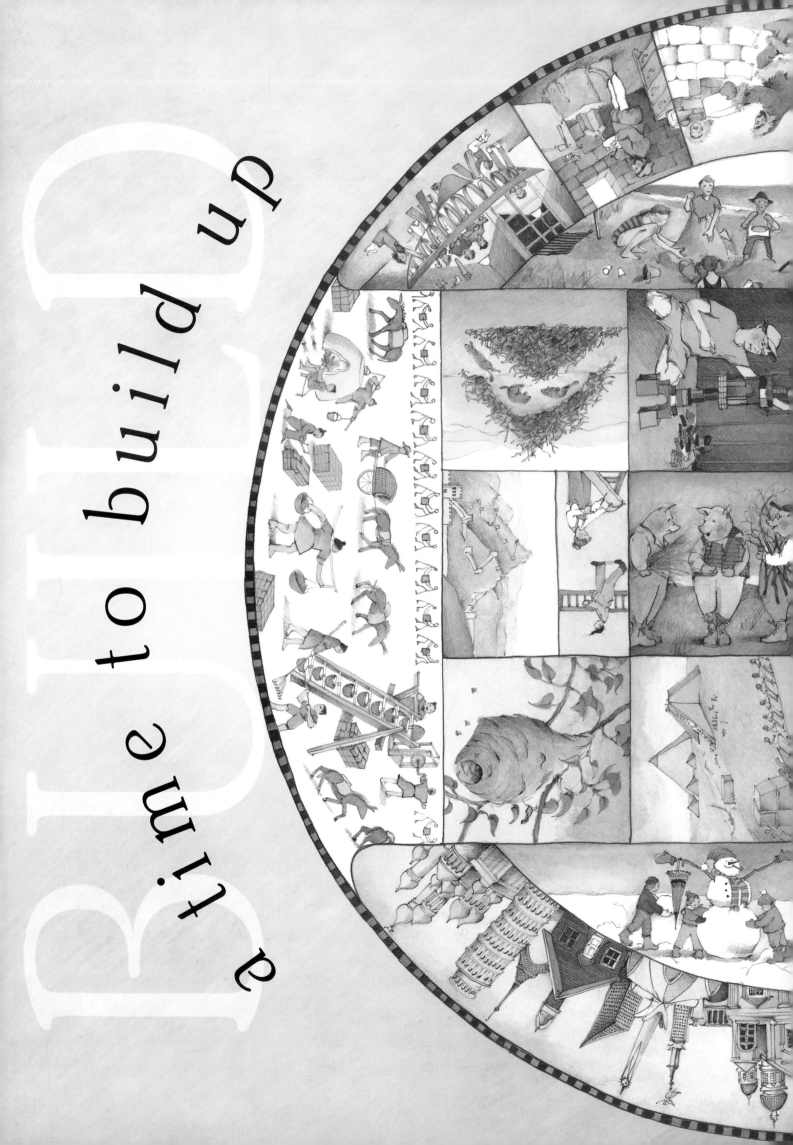

a time to break down

DANCE

a time to dance

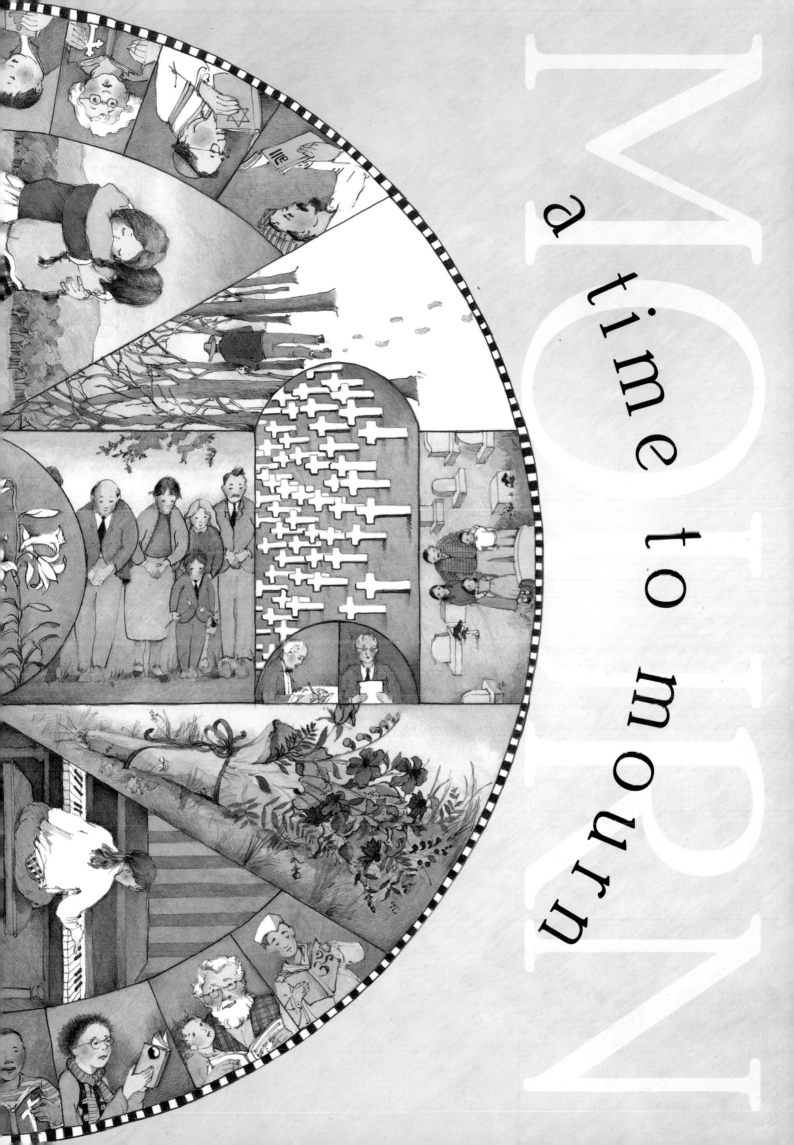

MOURN a time to mourn

a time to gather stones together

II

a time of hate

a time of peace

a time you may embrace

REFRAIN

a time to refrain from embracing

a time to gain

a time to lose

a time to sew

A time to love, a time to hate;

a time for peace, I swear it's not too late.

Suggestions for How to Use This Book

How was this song put together? Around 1961 I got a letter from my publisher, Howard Richmond, saying, "Pete, I love these protest songs you keep writing, but can't you write another song like 'Goodnight Irene'?" I was a little angry and sat down at a reel-to-reel tape recorder and spoke into the mike. "Howie, you better get yourself another songwriter. This is the only kind of song I know how to write."

I pulled a piece of paper out of my pocket on which I'd copied words from the Bible a few days before and started improvising an irregular melody for them. I rearranged the order of verses slightly so they'd rhyme a bit, and added six words of my own to complete a fourth verse. I found that the word "turn" repeated three times after a verse made a singable refrain. Then I sang it all into the tape recorder and mailed the tape. A few days later Howie wrote back: "Wonderful. Just what I was looking for." He got it to Roger McGuinn and the Byrds, who made history with it. My original tune and the Byrds' differ slightly. The main way the Byrds changed my melody is shown here in red. You sing it the way you want to. *That's the folk process!*

time for ev'ry pur-pose   laugh, — a time — to weep —.

Now a fantastic illustrator has made this book out of the song. How grateful I am to her; to book designer Greg Stadnyk; and to Jessica Schulte, our editor at Simon & Schuster. And though I don't usually feel grateful to corporations, I do feel grateful to Simon & Schuster for organizing things so that these words, music, and pictures hopefully will reach many people in many places.

Let's also thank the printers, papermakers, truckers, and salespeople who've done their jobs. Let's thank the trees, water, and sunlight.

My longtime aim has been to put songs on people's lips, not just in their ears. Let's encourage people to be participants, not just spectators, not just listeners, or even just readers. Ideally, books can help us be participants in trying to save this world from selfishness and shortsightedness.

And perhaps if more of us participate in trying to put together a world of some kind of peace and justice, then a century from now, there will still be a human race here. Competing, yes, but cooperating, too. Speaking out at times, but at other times keeping silent.

— Pete Seeger, 2003